To Ronald, who loves strawberry pie
D. D.

For Doug, Samantha, Carter, and Duffy
A. C.

Text copyright © 2007 by Dayle Ann Dodds
Illustrations copyright © 2007 by Abby Carter

First edition 2007

Library of Congress Cataloging-in-Publication Data
Dodds, Dayle Ann.
Full House : an invitation to fractions / Dayle Ann Dodds ; illustrated by Abby Carter. –1st ed.
p.   cm.
ISBN 978-0-7636-2468-2
1. Fractions – Juvenile literature.   I. Carter, Abby, ill. II. Title.
QA117.D63 2007
513.2'6 – dc22   2006051847

2 4 6 8 10 9 7 5 3 1

Printed in China

This book was typeset in Cafeteria.
The illustrations were done in watercolor and black colored pencil.

Candlewick Press
2067 Massachusetts Avenue
Cambridge, Massachusetts 02140

visit us at www.candlewick.com

Full House

An Invitation to Fractions

Dayle Ann Dodds

illustrated by
Abby Carter

CANDLEWICK PRESS
CAMBRIDGE, MASSACHUSETTS

The Strawberry Inn was run by Miss Bloom.
Happy was she to fill every room.

With one for herself and five for the guests,
there were six rooms in all for a cozy night's rest.

The
Strawberry Inn

VACANCY

Knock-knock!

went the door.

Ding-dong!

the bell rang.

"Welcome, welcome," Miss Bloom sang.

"Aye, a rest, that be my wish,"
said Sea Captain Duffy, who smelled just like fish.

So Sea Captain Duffy, all tired and done,
followed Miss Bloom to Room Number 1.

Now ONE room of SIX had a guest for the night.
To fill up the inn would be pure delight.

$\dfrac{1}{6}$

Knock-knock! went the door. *Ding-dong!* the bell rang.
"Welcome, welcome," Miss Bloom sang.

"Charmed, I'm sure," said the Duchess Boofaye.
"Smoochie and I are on holiday."

So the Duchess Boofaye, in sapphires of blue,
followed Miss Bloom to Room Number 2.

Now TWO rooms of SIX had guests for the night.
To fill up the inn would be pure delight!

$\dfrac{2}{6}$

Knock-knock! went the door. *Ding-dong!* the bell rang.
"Welcome, welcome," Miss Bloom sang.

"Care for a hairbrush, a toothbrush, a comb?
Or maybe a vacuum?" said Salesman Jerome.

Arms full of shoe polish, pots, pans, and tea,
he followed Miss Bloom to Room Number 3.

Now THREE rooms of SIX had guests for the night.
To fill up the inn would be pure delight!

$\frac{3}{6}$

Knock-knock! went the door. *Ding-dong!* the bell rang.
"Welcome, welcome," Miss Bloom sang.

"In town for my show!" said Trainer P. Klein.
From smallest to LARGEST, his dogs stood in line.

Then Trainer P. Klein and doggies galore
danced down the hall to Room Number 4.

Now FOUR rooms of SIX had guests for the night.
To fill up the inn would be pure delight!

$$\frac{4}{6}$$

Knock-knock! went the door. *Ding-dong!* the bell rang.
"Welcome, welcome," Miss Bloom sang.

"My biggest race ever!" said Johnny Z. Power.
"I hit two-hundred-ten miles per hour!"

Carrying his trophy and pleased to arrive,
he followed Miss Bloom to Room Number 5.

Five rooms of six had guests for the night,
filling Miss Bloom with pure delight.

$\dfrac{5}{6}$

Then into the kitchen Miss Bloom went to make
a scrumptious dinner for all to partake.

There were chicken and peas, potatoes au gratin,
but the very best part—
        Miss Bloom had forgotten!

A strawberry cake
    with whipped cream piled high
still sat on the counter
    when the last dish was dry.

Tired and happy, they all went to bed—
Miss Bloom in Room 6.
"It's a FULL HOUSE," she said.

$$\frac{6}{6} = 1$$

The guests and Miss Bloom all called out,

"Good night!"

plumped up
each pillow,

and
turned off
each light.

But then, in the dark, came shuffles and wiggles,
whispers and mumbles, scuffles and giggles.

Shadows were tiptoeing down the long hall.
But where were they going, bathrobes and all?

Suddenly, Miss Bloom sat up in bed.
"Something's not right at my inn," she said.

She rushed to the kitchen and turned on the light.
There she saw an astonishing sight:

Five out of six–

and the dogs and the cat–

stood covered in cake from toe to top hat.

"Well!" said Miss Bloom, and "Tiddle-ee-dee!

Thank you for saving the last piece

FOR ME!"

$\frac{1}{6}$

$\frac{1}{6}$

$\frac{1}{6}$

$\frac{1}{6}$

$\frac{1}{6}$

$\frac{1}{6}$

$$\frac{6}{6} = 1$$